D1128443

Mary K. Pershall
'Hello, BARNEY!'
illustrated by Mark Wilson

Viking Kestrel

Viking Kestrel, an imprint of Penguin Books Ltd
Melbourne, London, New York, Auckland
First published 1988
First American edition published in 1989
Copyright © Mary K. Pershall, 1988. Illustrations copyright © Mark Wilson, 1988
Made and printed in Singapore by Kyodo Printing Co. Ltd.

Long ago, before airplanes flew in the Australian sky,
a pair of cockatoos watched over their clutch of eggs.

One day as the sun rose
to light the bush in green and gold,
the three eggs hatched.

One of the nestlings was a male. From the moment of his hatching he ate up everything his parents had to offer, and he grew quickly. By the time he was eight days old his baby fluff had begun to change into feathers, and at the end of two months he was ready to leave the nest.

He was ready to leave the nest,
but he was inexperienced.
He was young and greedy and curious.
He found a line of seeds scattered on the ground,
and he didn't know enough to be suspicious.

He gobbled up the tasty seeds,
one after another . . .
and walked right into a trap.
The door clanged shut behind him.

At first there was only rage inside the trap,
and the red hot throbbing feel of panic.

And pain –
from his young wings beating against the wire,
and from his heart, pounding and pounding and pounding.

At last he lay exhausted in the bottom of the cage,
too tired to fight.

He became aware of a sound:
a low, soothing sound.
'Barney. Barney,' said the sound.
'It's all right. No one's going to hurt you.
You're mine now, Barney.'

It was the voice of a boy.

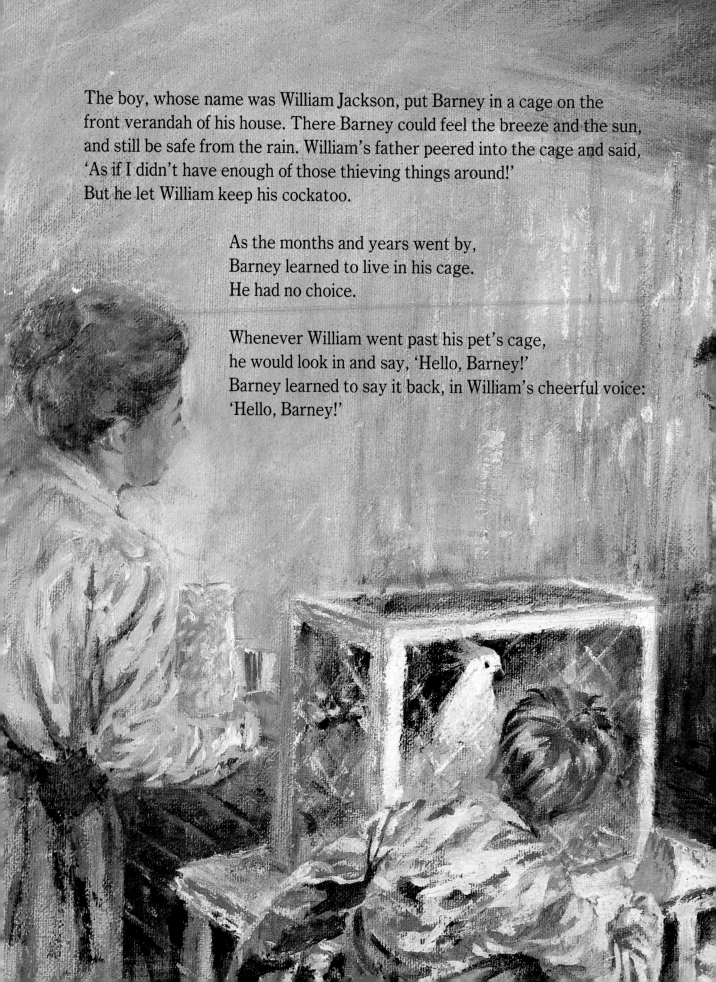

The boy, whose name was William Jackson, put Barney in a cage on the front verandah of his house. There Barney could feel the breeze and the sun, and still be safe from the rain. William's father peered into the cage and said, 'As if I didn't have enough of those thieving things around!'
But he let William keep his cockatoo.

As the months and years went by,
Barney learned to live in his cage.
He had no choice.

Whenever William went past his pet's cage,
he would look in and say, 'Hello, Barney!'
Barney learned to say it back, in William's cheerful voice:
'Hello, Barney!'

When William Jackson grew up, he went to the city and found a job.
He liked the city. Yet every day he thought of a cage with a cockatoo inside
on a certain front verandah.

William married about the time that Barney might have taken a mate, had he still been free in the bush. As soon as William and his wife had saved enough money to buy a house, William fetched Barney from the farm.

'That squawking will drive me mad!' said Mrs Jennifer Jackson.
'Now don't you whine,' said William. 'A man needs a little bit of nature.'

In the Jacksons' back garden,
summer heat followed winter rain,
year after year after year.

Two small humans arrived.

Kittens grew up and had kittens
of their own.

Barney watched it all.

William kept one of Barney's wings clipped, so that he could only fly
in little jerky circles like a crippled bird. He didn't want him to fly away.
This didn't matter much to Barney, as he couldn't remember what it had
been like to really fly.

During those family years, the children had a dog called Heidi.
Sometimes they put Barney on Heidi's back, for a joke.
Heidi would look disgusted, but she never shook Barney off.

In the Jacksons' back garden, winter rain followed summer sun,
year after year after year.

The girls grew tall but still liked to play in the shed next to Barney's cage.
There was a hole in the shed that was just the right size for a cockatoo's eye.
The girls never knew that Barney watched everything they did.

Long after the girls had stopped playing in the shed,
long after Heidi had been buried under the ghost gum,
Barney still watched his garden, and all that happened there.

For cockatoos live a long, long time.

There are not many animals who live as long as cockies do.
Elephants can, and giant tortoises. And sometimes humans.

William Jackson was one of those humans who live a long, long time.
He changed a lot more than Barney did. His blue eyes grew milky.
His skin was dry and wrinkled. His legs began to hurt him when he walked.

Yet William loved his boyhood pet as much as ever. Sometimes as a treat,
William gave Barney a drumstick, left over from a fried chicken.
William would say, 'You like that, don't you? You old cannibal!'

William sat in a chair that he kept beside Barney's cage.
He often talked to Barney just to pass the time:
'You're about the only family I got left now. Good thing
I got you locked up! I don't like that house much any more –
seems like it's gone sort of dark.'

'The girls . . . I know they got their own lives to lead.
When their mother was alive they used to come around a bit,
but I guess they're too busy to be bothered with us now.'

Many times, Barney and William would go to sleep
in the sunlight in their garden. Then they would dream.
Some dreams they dreamed together, while others came
from deep inside their separate heads.

There came a morning at the end of
winter. Barney sat huddled in his cage,
waiting for William Jackson.

But William did not come.

Watery sunlight passed over the garden
and still William didn't come, not until
it was almost dark. At last the old man
shuffled out – slowly, slowly –
to feed his cockatoo.

William didn't say much, but he
scratched the tender spot
under Barney's sulphur crest.
And when he left Barney,
William did something he had never
done before:
he left the cage door open.

The sun rose and set, rose and set
again, but Barney stayed in his cage.
Cockatoos, like humans, find habits
hard to break.

Finally, when the rain had stopped and
the sun lit up the garden with an early
spring rainbow, hunger drove Barney
from his cage.

Barney picked at the grass, but there weren't many seeds in it this time of year. He walked around to the front of the house. The house looked dark and empty.

Barney didn't see the dog rush up from behind him, but he must have heard it, or sensed it.

Barney jumped, flapped his wings, and rose from the ground. Higher and higher he rose in the air. An old sensation filled his brain and body. He was soaring, gliding on the currents. He could see for miles. For the first time in seventy years, Barney flew.

It had been a long time since William had bothered to clip Barney's wing.
Now Barney flew like the cockatoo he was meant to be.

But Barney was weak from hunger, and he was old.
His muscles weren't used to flying. When he grew so tired
that he couldn't fly on a second longer, he landed on top
of a pole.

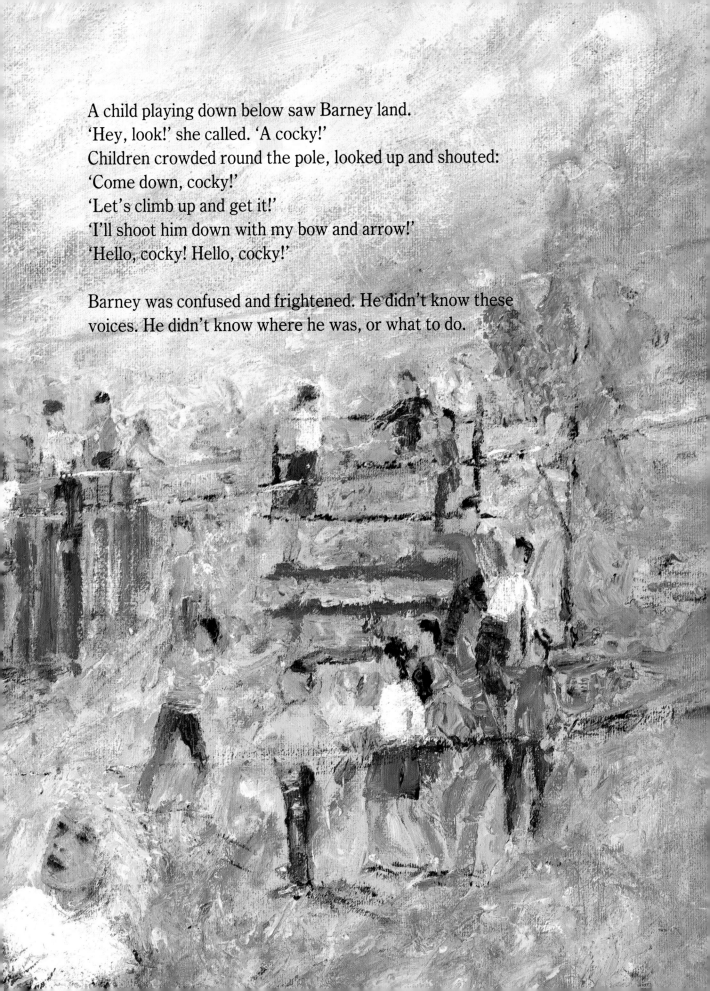

A child playing down below saw Barney land.
'Hey, look!' she called. 'A cocky!'
Children crowded round the pole, looked up and shouted:
'Come down, cocky!'
'Let's climb up and get it!'
'I'll shoot him down with my bow and arrow!'
'Hello, cocky! Hello, cocky!'

Barney was confused and frightened. He didn't know these
voices. He didn't know where he was, or what to do.

Gradually the children lost interest and drifted away – except for one.
From her came a soft, soothing sound:
'Come on down now, cocky. I won't hurt you. Come on down to me.'

Her voice reminded Barney of a voice he'd known.

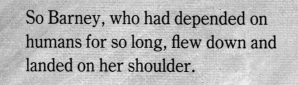

So Barney, who had depended on
humans for so long, flew down and
landed on her shoulder.

'Nobody's going to hurt you,' said the
girl, as she scratched underneath the
sulphur crest. 'We'll go into Dad now
and get you some food.'

Barney cocked his head at her.
With William Jackson's cheerful voice
he said:
'Hello, Barney!'